The Christmas Boot

by Lisa Wheeler

illustrated by Jerry Pinkney

Dial Books for Young Readers

Deep in the forest on Christmas morning, Hannah Greyweather gathered bundles of kindling wood. For her, this day was no different from any other. As she went about her chores, she chatted to the forest, she talked to the mountains, but mostly she spoke to herself.

"Brrrrr," she said to the mountain. "Will this winter ever be over? It chills my bones."

The mountain didn't answer.

Her arms were nearly full when, just past the spruce grove, she spotted something. In the snow, deepest black upon purest white, lay a boot.

"Glory be!" Hannah exclaimed to the forest. "Who could've lost this?"

The forest remained silent.

And since her feet were fully freezing, and since it looked to be such a nice boot, she slipped her rag-wrapped left foot deep within it.

"Ahhh," Hannah said. "That does feel nice."

It surely must have, for when she slid her tiny foot into the very large boot, it suddenly took on the shape and size of Hannah's own foot. The boot fit perfectly.

Hannah headed back to her ramshackle cabin, limping her way through the snow. Her warm left foot stepped nimbly as her cold right foot struggled to keep up.

"This boot was quite a find," Hannah said to the walls of her cabin. "Where do you suppose it came from?"

The walls did not reply.

As she slipped into bed that night, she stared at
the boot and said, "I only wish I had your mate."
Then she drifted off to sleep.

"Come on, boot," Hannah said the next morning. "Time to get to work." But as she slid her legs over the side of the bed, she didn't see just one black boot. She saw two!

"Glory be!" Hannah said to the right boot. "How did *you* get here?"

The boot didn't say.

Then Hannah Greyweather placed both her feet into those warm black boots. They fit most comfortably.

As she went about her wood-gathering, Hannah had a spring in her step that hadn't been there for years. She danced in the spruce grove, skipped along the creek bed, and even made snow angels on the hillside. Her feet felt wonderfully warm.

That night, Hannah placed her boots next to her bed and marveled at her good fortune.

"Such a magnificent find," she said to the left boot. "Who could have lost such a treasure as you?"

The boot stood silent.

"No matter," said Hannah. "I've made good use of you. If I had mittens as toasty warm, I would be the happiest woman in the world."

In the morning, tucked neatly inside each boot was a bright red mitten.

"Glory be!" Hannah said to the boots. "What form of magic is this?"

The boots wouldn't tell.

She put on the mittens, and like the boots, they fit perfectly.

"If the boot is magic," Hannah said to the mittens, "will it give me more? Will it give me a fluffy feather bed? A fabulous feast? A big fancy house?"

The mittens stayed mute.

"I suppose that is too much to ask," said Hannah. "I best get about my chores."

In the woods that day, Hannah's feet
and hands felt equally fine. She climbed
the mountain trail, gathered chestnuts, and
built a towering snowman.

As she strolled home, an amazing
sight met her eyes.

Where her ramshackle cabin had been stood a big fancy house. Luscious smells drifted from the open doorway.

"Glory be!" Hannah said to the house. "How did you get here?"

The house didn't say.

Inside, Hannah wandered from room to room, taking in the loveliness of it all. She tasted the fabulous foods, she snuggled in the fluffy feather bed. Somehow, it didn't seem fully real.

It didn't seem fully right, either. Unlike the wonderful boots and mittens, the house didn't seem to "fit" Hannah.

Suddenly, there came a *KNOCK-KNOCK-KNOCK* on the fine front door. "Who could it be?" Hannah asked the feather bed. "I've never had company." The bed stayed silent.

She opened the door cautiously. Peeking through the crack between the door and the wall, she spied a man with a very white beard. He wore a red hat, a red suit . . . and one black boot.

"May I help you?" Hannah asked the man.

"Yes," he answered. "I think you may have found something of mine."

Hannah was happily surprised to hear the sound of another voice. She opened the door at once. "Glory be!" she said. "Come in, come in! You must be freezing."

"Just my left foot," said the man, with a twinkle in his eye.

Hannah looked down at her own booted feet. "Yes," she said. "I do believe I have something that belongs to you."

She fixed the man a cup of tea. She served him chestnuts. They talked of everything and nothing, deep into the night.

"Now," she said, "I best give you your boot, so you can be on your way."

When the man placed his large left foot into the boot, it took on the shape and size of his very own foot.

"Ahhh," he said. "That does feel nice."

At once, the big fancy house, the fabulous feast, and the fluffy feather bed disappeared. Even her right boot and mittens were gone.

"I am sorry," said the man.

"No need," said Hannah. "It is as it should be. The boot didn't belong to me, but I enjoyed it while it was here."

"Is there anything I can give you?" asked the man. "What do you truly desire?"

"What I truly desire is someone to talk to," said Hannah. "But warm boots and a pair of mittens would be mighty fine."

The man in the red suit winked. Suddenly, there appeared a dandy pair of red boots and bright green mittens.

"Thank you, sir," Hannah said as she walked him to the door and bid him good-bye. "I will make fine use of them."

That night as she climbed into bed, Hannah said "Good night" to her new mittens and boots.

"Arf!" the left boot answered.

"What?!" Hannah cried. She peeked inside the boot. Two eyes peered back at her.

"Arf! Arf!" she heard again. Then she reached into the boot, and pulled a wiggly puppy into her arms.

"Thank you," Hannah whispered to the night sky as she held her new friend close.

The night sky answered . . .

"Merry Christmas, Hannah! Merry Christmas!"

In loving memory of Linda Smith. I wrote this one for her. —L.W.

To my aunt Edna, whose spirit and smile are all inspiring. —J.P.

Dial Books for Young Readers

Penguin Young Readers Group

An imprint of Penguin Random House LLC

375 Hudson Street

New York, NY 10014

Library of Congress Cataloging-in-Publication Data

Names: Wheeler, Lisa, date, author. | Pinkney, Jerry, illustrator.

Title: The Christmas boot / by Lisa Wheeler ; illustrated by Jerry Pinkney.

Description: New York, NY : Dial Books for Young Readers, [2016] |

Summary: Hannah Greyweather's life is changed when she finds a
magic wish-granting boot in the forest outside her home.

Identifiers: LCCN 2015022344 | ISBN 9780803741348 (hardcover)

Subjects: | CYAC: Christmas—Fiction. | Magic—Fiction. | Wishes—Fiction. |
Santa Claus—Fiction.

Classification: LCC PZ7.W5657 Chr 2016 | DDC [E]—dc23

LC record available at http://lccn.loc.gov/2015022344

Printed in China

3 5 7 9 10 8 6 4 2

Design by Lily Malcom • Text set in Stempel Garamond

The art was created using pencil, Prismacolor pencils, and watercolor on Arches cold press watercolor paper.

21982319335471

FREDERICK COUNTY PUBLIC LIBRARIES

DEC   2019